The New Boy

The New Boy

HOLLY KELLER

Red Fox

to JC, KH,
MH, MJ, GM,
SM, TM,
and MO

A Red Fox Book

Published by Random House Children's Books
20 Vauxhall Bridge Road, London SW1V 2SA

A division of Random House UK Ltd
London Melbourne Sydney Auckland
Johannesburg and agencies throughout the world

First published in the USA by Greenwillow Books 1991
First published in Great Britain by Julia MacRae 1991

Red Fox edition 1994

© Holly Keller 1991

Printed in China

RANDOM HOUSE UK Limited Reg. No. 9544009

ISBN 0 09 910871 2

The day Miss Higgins introduced Milton to the class,
he stuck out his tongue, and everybody laughed.

"Let's welcome Milton," Miss Higgins said with a smile,
and she patted him on the head.
"The new boy is weird," Judy whispered to Marge.
And Marge passed it on.

At midday there was a caterpillar in Mindy's lunch box.
"Milton did it," Mindy shrieked, and she screamed until
her face was nearly purple.

The next day Milton knocked down Timmy's castle.
There were blocks all over the floor.

Molly slipped on one and skidded into the easel.
Then she cried until it was time for lunch.

When Gregory brought special cupcakes for a snack,
Milton picked off all the cherries. Gregory had a fit.
"I hope you throw up!" he yelled.

And Milton had to clean the art table to make up for it.

Each day Milton did more bad things.
He jumped out of the coat cupboard and scared
Miss Higgins half to death,

he sang during rest time,

and he wouldn't share anything.

"You're BAD," Henry said, and Milton began to cry.
Everyone was too surprised to speak.

The next week Milton was a perfect angel.
When Miss Higgins made him a captain for football,
Milton shook his head.
"I'll stay inside and water the plants," he said.

Then he started to put away all the blocks and cars.
"Wait," Timmy shouted. "That's our city!"
But Milton was too busy to hear.

When everyone was having ice-cream,
Milton said he'd clean the turtle tank.

It took all morning to get the turtles back,
and Miss Higgins had to cancel music.
But she said "Thank you" to Milton, anyway.

Each day Milton did more good things.
He volunteered to mix the paints,

he cleaned the dusters,

he washed the floor,

and he wouldn't whisper to anyone at rest time.

Now everyone was really MAD.
Gregory whispered to Marge, and Mindy agreed,
"This is worse than when he was bad!"

Stanley arrived that afternoon.
Miss Higgins showed him around.
"Let's welcome Stanley," she said to the class,
and Stanley covered his ears. He crossed his eyes
and shuffled his feet, and Henry laughed out loud.

"The new boy is weird,"
Molly whispered to Milton.

And Milton passed it on.

The next day Milton came to school singing
a little song. He hung up his coat, put away
his lunch, and settled down to play.